This book belongs to:

_____

_____

Written by Jillian Harker
Illustrated by Kristina Stephenson

First published 2008 Parragon Books, Ltd.

Copyright © 2018 Cottage Door Press, LLC
5005 Newport Drive, Rolling Meadows, Illinois 60008
All Rights Reserved

ISBN: 978-1-68052-426-0

Parragon Books is an imprint
of Cottage Door Press, LLC.
Parragon Books® and the Parragon® logo are
registered trademarks of Cottage Door Press, LLC.

I Love You, Daddy

"You're getting tall, Little Bear," said Daddy Bear. "Big enough to come climbing with me." Little Bear's eyes opened wide in surprise.

"Do you really mean that?" said Little Bear. Daddy Bear nodded. He led Little Bear to a giant tree.

Little Bear tried to scramble
up onto the lowest branch.

He tumbled backward.

Daddy Bear
nudged
Little Bear.

Daddy Bear
tugged
Little Bear.

"You can do it!" he whispered.

And suddenly, Little Bear found that he could.
"I love Daddy," thought Little Bear.

"You're getting brave, Little Bear," said
Daddy Bear. "Daring enough to gather
honey with me."
Little Bear gasped.
   "Could I really?"
Daddy Bear winked.
He led Little Bear to
another tree and pointed
to a hole in the trunk.

Little Bear reached out his paw.
A furious buzzing filled his ears.
Little Bear pulled his paw back.

Buzz!

Buzz!

Buzz!

Buzz!

"Just be quick," Daddy Bear said. "You have thick fur. The bees can't hurt you. You can do it!" he smiled.

And suddenly, Little Bear found that he could.

"I love Daddy," thought Little Bear.

"You're getting smart, Little Bear. Smart enough to find a good winter den."
Little Bear grinned.

"Do you really think so?"

"I know so," said Daddy Bear.

Little Bear set off.
"Not too far from food," said Daddy
Bear. "Ready for when spring comes."
Little Bear sniffed the wind.

"Look for high ground," said
Daddy Bear, "to keep us dry."
Little Bear padded up
over the rocks.

"Somewhere safe and
warm," said Daddy Bear,
"away from danger."

"Here!" called Little Bear as he disappeared into a deep cave.

Daddy Bear followed. He looked all around.
"Perfect!" he said.
"I love Daddy," thought Little Bear.

"Did I climb well?" Little Bear asked on the way home.

"You did!" replied Daddy Bear.

"Was I brave?" asked Little Bear.

"You were!" answered Daddy Bear.

"Did I find a good den?" asked Little Bear.

"The very best!" smiled Daddy Bear. "I'm proud of you, Little Bear."

Soon Little Bear and Daddy Bear reached home.
And suddenly, Little Bear felt very tired,
but there was something he wanted to say.

"I love you, D..." began Little Bear.
But he didn't finish.

Daddy Bear stroked Little Bear's head.
"I love you, too," he said.